W9-BZH-732

WITHDRAWN
BY
WILLIAMSBURG REGIONAL LIBRARY

OCT - - 2018

Copyright © 2018 by Geraldo Valério
Published in Canada and the USA in 2018 by Groundwood Books

All rights reserved. No part of this publication may be reproduced, stored in a retrieval system or transmitted, in any form or by any means, without the prior written consent of the publisher or a license from The Canadian Copyright Licensing Agency (Access Copyright). For an Access Copyright license, visit www.accesscopyright.ca or call toll free to 1-800-893-5777.

Groundwood Books / House of Anansi Press
groundwoodbooks.com

We acknowledge for their financial support of our publishing program the Canada Council for the Arts, the Ontario Arts Council and the Government of Canada.

Canada Council for the Arts | Conseil des Arts du Canada

ONTARIO ARTS COUNCIL
CONSEIL DES ARTS DE L'ONTARIO
an Ontario government agency
un organisme du gouvernement de l'Ontario

With the participation of the Government of Canada
Avec la participation du gouvernement du Canada | Canada

Library and Archives Canada Cataloguing in Publication

Valério, Geraldo, author, illustrator
Blue rider / Geraldo Valério.

Issued in print and electronic formats.
ISBN 978-1-55498-981-2 (hardcover). – ISBN 978-1-55498-982-9 (PDF)

I. Title.

PS8643.A422B58 2018 jC813'.6 C2017-905230-6
C2017-905231-4

The illustrations were created with pen and color-pencil drawing, acrylic paint and collage.
Design by Michael Solomon
Printed and bound in Malaysia

FSC
www.fsc.org
MIX
Paper from responsible sources
FSC® C012700

BLUE RIDER

GERALDO VALÉRIO

WILLIAMSBURG REGIONAL LIBRARY
7770 CROAKER ROAD
WILLIAMSBURG, VA 23188

GROUNDWOOD BOOKS
HOUSE OF ANANSI PRESS
TORONTO BERKELEY

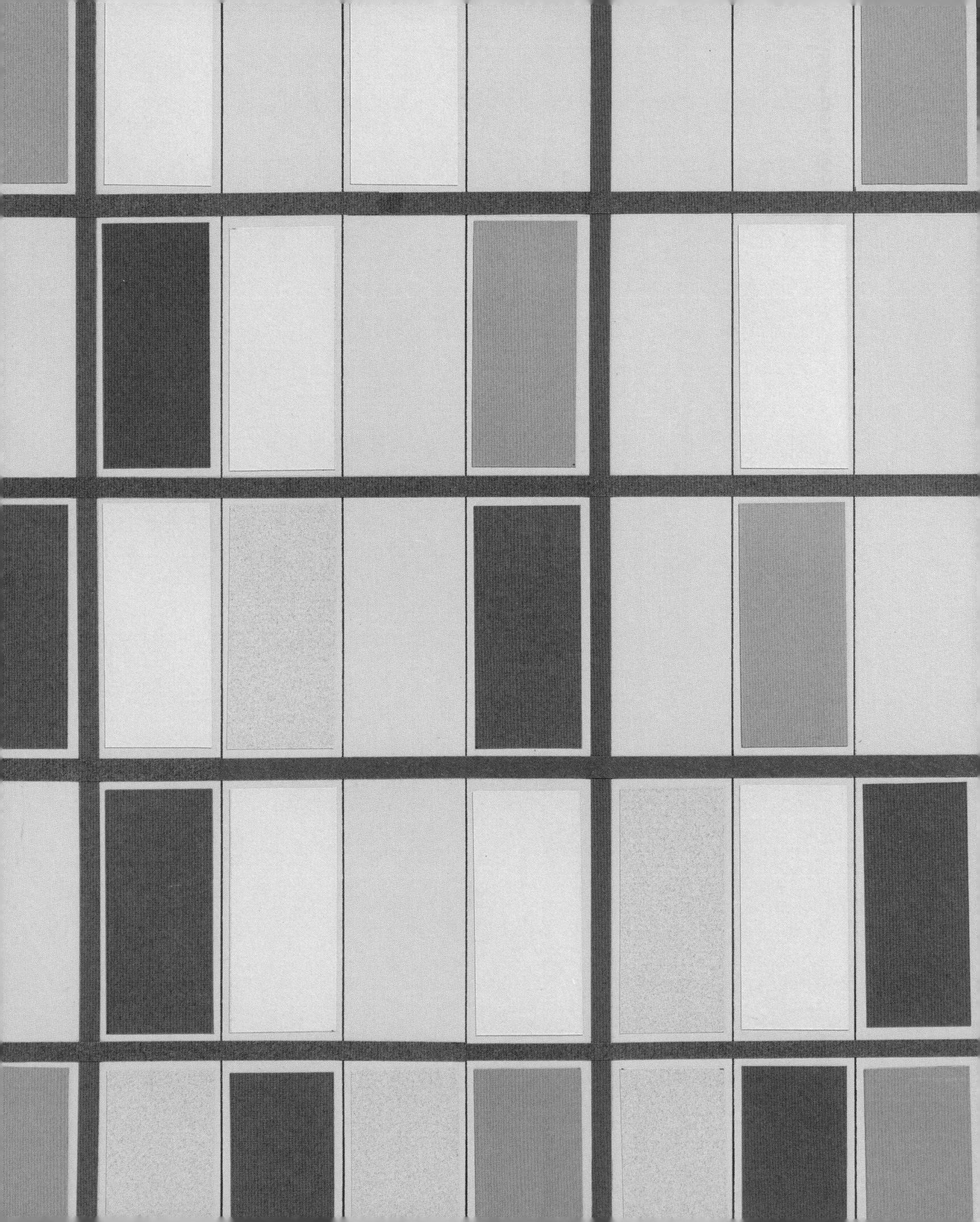